Steadwell Books World Tour

FRANCE

CHRISTOPHER MITTEN

Steadwell
Books

Raintree Steck-Vaughn Publishers
A Harcourt Company

Austin · New York
www.raintreesteckvaughn.com

Published by Raintree Steck-Vaughn Publishers, an imprint of Steck-Vaughn Company

Editor: Simone T. Ribke
Designer: Maria E. Torres

Library of Congress Cataloging-in-Publication Data
Mitten, Christopher.
   France / Christopher Mitten.
      p. cm. -- (Steadwell books world tour)
   Includes bibliographical references (p.) and index.
   Summary: Describes the history, geography, economy, government, religious and social life, culture, various famous people, and outstanding tourist sites of France. Includes a recipe for chocolate mousse.
   ISBN 0-7398-5753-3
      1. France--Juvenile literature. [1. France.] I. Title. II. Series.

   DC17 .M57 2002
   941.4--dc21   2002017873

Printed in the United States of America
1 2 3 4 5 6 7 8 9 10 WZ 05 04 03 02

Photo acknowledgments
Cover (a) ©eStock; cover (b) ©Patrick Ingrand/Getty Images; cover (c) ©Euan Myles/ Getty Images; p.1a ©Richard T. Nowitz; p.1b ©eStock; p.1c ©SuperStock; p.3a ©Becky Luigart-Stayner/CORBIS; p.3b ©Gail Mooney/CORBIS; p.5 ©SuperStock; p.6 ©AKG Berlin/SuperStock; p.7 ©Charles Graham/eStock; p.8 ©AFP/CORBIS; p.13a ©Adam Woolfitt/CORBIS; p.13b ©SIME/ eStock ; p.14 ©Dalmasso/ImageState; p.15 ©Patrick Ingrand/Getty Images; p.16 ©Steve Vidler/ SuperStock; p.17 ©eStock; p.19 ©Murat Ayranci/SuperStock; p.21 ©Adam Woolfitt/CORBIS; p.22 ©Archivo Iconografico/CORBIS; p.23 ©Charles E. Rotkin/CORBIS; p.24 ©Gail Mooney/ CORBIS p.25 ©AFP/CORBIS; p.27a ©eStock; p.27b Marc Garanger/CORBIS; p.28 ©Beryl Goldberg; p.29 ©AFP/CORBIS; p.31a ©Reuters NewMedia Inc/CORBIS; p.31b ©Owen Franken/ CORBIS; p.33 ©David Warren/SuperStock; p.34 ©Owen Franken/CORBIS; p.35 ©Michael Boys/ CORBIS; p.37 ©Sandro Vannini/CORBIS; p.39 ©Brian Leatart/FoodPix; p.40 ©AFP/CORBIS; p.41 ©Anne B. Keiser/SuperStock; p.42 ©Steve Vidler/SuperStock; p.43b ©Gail Mooney/ CORBIS; p.43c ©Premium Stock/CORBIS; p.44a ©Rufus F Folkks/CORBIS; p.44b,c ©Bettmann/ CORBIS.

CONTENTS

Welcome to France

Are you thinking about making a trip to France? Maybe you want to find out more about this incredible country. Perhaps you like reading about historic battles, amazing art, and wonderful food. Whatever your reason for picking up this book, you will discover that the story of France is thrilling. France has a long history, a beautiful landscape, and countless fascinating people. Ready to take a tour? Read on!

A Tip to Get You Started

- *Look at the Pictures*

This book has lots of great photos. Flip through and check out those pictures you like the best. This is a quick way to get an idea of what this book is all about. Read the captions to learn even more about the photos.

- *Use the Glossary*

As you read this book, you may notice that some words appear in **bold** print. Look up bold words in the Glossary at the back of the book. The Glossary will help you learn what they mean.

- *Use the Index*

If you are looking for a certain fact on France, then you might want to go to the Index, also at the back of the book. There you'll find a list of all the subjects covered in the book.

▲ VINEYARDS IN MARANGES, FRANCE
France is known for its amazing wines. And Maranges,
France, is where some of the most beautiful grape vineyards
are found. As you stroll through the hills, you can smell the
grapes.

FRANCE'S PAST

The history of France is filled with great stories of wars and battles, kings, queens, an emperor, and a revolution.

Ancient History

A Celtic people called the Gauls were the earliest known **ancestors** of modern-day French people. The Gauls arrived about 1500 B.C. By A.D. 400, tribes from the east began raiding Gaul. The most powerful tribe was the Franks. They quickly took over. The region has been known as France ever since.

In the centuries that followed, five important **dynasties** ruled France. The last, and most important, was the Bourbon dynasty. The first Bourbon king was Henry of Navarre. He ended centuries of bitter religious wars between Catholics and Protestants. King Louis XIV ("XIV" means the 14th) was the most important Bourbon king. He was often called the "Sun King." He ruled from 1643 to 1715. Under his rule, France enjoyed its Golden Age. It also became the greatest power in Europe.

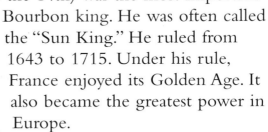

◄ **PLACE DES PYRAMIDES**
This statue of Joan of Arc is located in downtown Paris. Joan of Arc, at age 17, led the French army to victory against the enemy in the 1400s. She was captured and burned at the stake in 1431.

The French Revolution and Napoleon

In 1789, the French **Revolution** began. The French people were sick of supporting a king and his very expensive court.

They created a new government. This led to a period of political violence known as the Reign of Terror. Thousands were executed on the **guillotine**.

Then a young, brilliant general named Napoleon Bonaparte took control and ended The Terror. In 1804 he declared himself the country's emperor. Napoleon conquered most of Europe. He was defeated at the battle of Waterloo in 1815.

France in the 19th Century

After Napoleon, France struggled to find a **stable** form of government. In 1871, democracy was restored.

During this period, many changes took place. Huge factories, railroads, and banks were built all over France. People moved to the city to work in factories rather than on farms. French literature and art began to explore realism and **Impressionism**, with thrilling results.

The World Wars

Sadly, the good times at the end of the 19th century did not last for long. In 1914, Europe plunged into troubled times that began with The Great War, or World War I.

This war lasted from 1914 to 1918. France, Britain, the United States, and Russia formed an **alliance** on one side. The Austrians and Germans were on the other. World War I was bloodier than any war had ever been. Over one million French soldiers died. Another million were wounded.

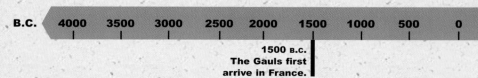

B.C.	4000	3500	3000	2500	2000	1500	1000	500	0

1500 B.C.
The Gauls first
arrive in France.

France and its allies won the war. But Europe was a disaster scene. By the mid-1930s, France experienced the effects of a worldwide **economic depression**. In Germany, the Nazi leader Adolf Hitler rose to power. He promised revenge for Germany's defeat and a solution to the Depression. Hitler blamed Europe's Jews for Germany's problems. In 1939, Hitler's invasion of Poland began World War II.

As in World War I, France allied with Great Britain, Russia, and the U.S. against Germany. But Germany invaded and defeated France in 1940. During the war, the Nazis killed more than six million European Jews. Around 75,000 of these victims were French.

Recent Times

When World War II ended, France formed a democratic government. In the years after the war, France had one major issue: What would be the future of its **foreign** colonies, such as Vietnam, Algeria, and Senegal, in Africa and the Far East? By the 1970s, France's colonies had become independent. Now, France is one of the most stable and prosperous nations in the world. Its future looks even brighter.

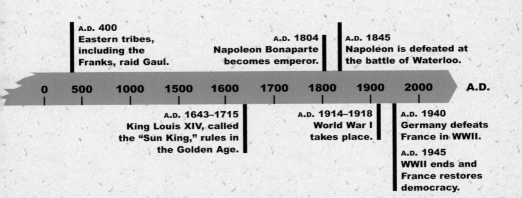

A.D. 400
Eastern tribes, including the Franks, raid Gaul.

A.D. 1804
Napoleon Bonaparte becomes emperor.

A.D. 1845
Napoleon is defeated at the battle of Waterloo.

0   500   1000   1500   1600   1700   1800   1900   2000   A.D.

A.D. 1643–1715
King Louis XIV, called the "Sun King," rules in the Golden Age.

A.D. 1914–1918
World War I takes place.

A.D. 1940
Germany defeats France in WWII.

A.D. 1945
WWII ends and France restores democracy.

A LOOK AT FRANCE'S GEOGRAPHY

Looking for a place that has it all? Then France may be the country for you. Its mountain ranges contain some of Europe's highest peaks. Its coastlines are popular hangouts for the rich and famous. Inland, you will find fertile farmland. This country has every landscape a traveler could want to see. Want more details? Read on.

Land

There are three main mountain ranges in France. The Pyrenees Mountains lie to the south and separate France from Spain. To the east stand the Jura Mountains along the border of Switzerland. Southeast of the Jura are the Alps. Mont Blanc, the tallest mountain in France, is part of the Alps. It stands 15,771 feet (4,807 m) high.

The rest of France is mostly flat land. Much of this is used for farming. Over 90% of French land is fertile. This means that there are lots of nutrients in the soil, so farmers have plenty to work with. In the north, the plains are wet and rich with **vegetation**. In the middle, the plains are drier and less fertile, although there are still many farms. In southwest France you will find fertile, wet lowlands. This land is perfect for growing grapes.

FRANCE'S SIZE ▶
France is the largest country in Western Europe. Its total area is 213,000 square miles (551,000 sq km). France borders on Spain, Andorra, Italy, Switzerland, Germany, and Luxembourg. Great Britain lies across the English Channel.

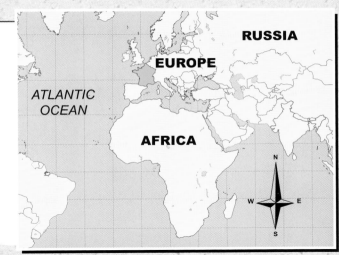

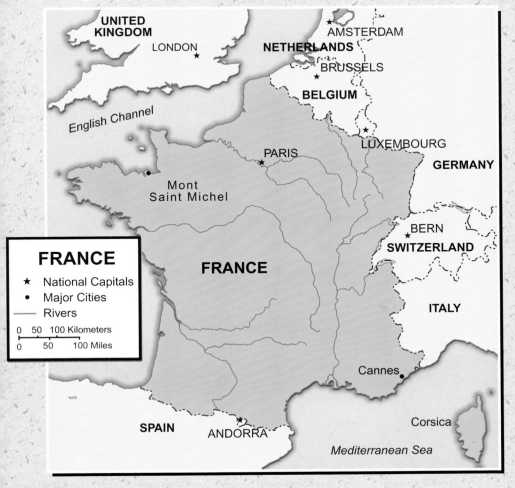

Water

Four main bodies of water surround France. To the west lies the Bay of Biscay, which is part of the Atlantic Ocean. To the south lies the Mediterranean Sea. To the north is the English Channel, and at the northeast tip is the North Sea. Altogether, France has about 2,000 miles (3,200 km) of coastline.

Rivers also play a major role in France's geography. France's longest river is the Loire. It stretches for about 640 miles (1,020 km). The Rhine River marks the border between France and Germany. Another major river in France is the Rhône. This river runs south from the Alps to the Mediterranean. The famous Seine River runs through Paris, France's capital.

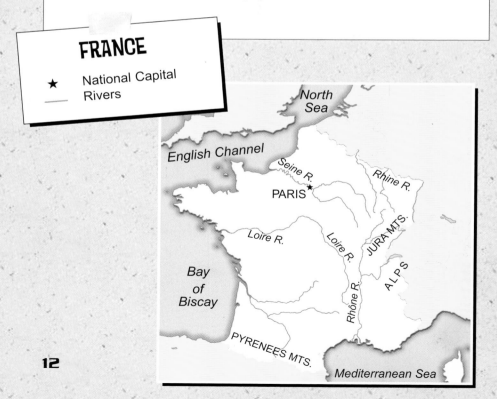

FRANCE

★ National Capital

— Rivers

North Sea

English Channel

Seine R.

PARIS ★

Rhine R.

Loire R.

Loire R.

JURA MTS.

Bay of Biscay

Rhône R.

ALPS

PYRENEES MTS.

Mediterranean Sea

▲ LOIRE RIVER
Did you know that the Loire is the last wild river in Western Europe? It flows naturally and has no man-made structures like dams.

ON THE BEACH IN CORSICA ▶
Hanging out at the beach takes on a whole new meaning in Corsica. This lovely French island is home to some of the most magnificent ocean views.

Weather

France lies midway between the **equator** and the
North Pole. It has a temperate climate, which means
that it is not too hot and not too cold. Of course,
weather varies from place to place. But there are no
tropical rain forests or polar bears.

The coldest place in France is the area around Mont
Blanc in the Alps. Glaciers surround it. Glaciers are
permanent fields of ice.

The warmest place is France's Mediterranean coast.
Average high temperatures reach about 83 degrees
Fahrenheit (28° C) in the summer. In the winter, it stays
around 53 degrees Fahrenheit (12° C).

Paris, the capital, is a little cooler than the coast. In
the winter, the highs average around 40 degrees
Fahrenheit (4° C). In the summer, they reach the mid
70s (around 24° C).

▲ DON'T BRUISE THE GRAPES!
This man from Vaucluse, France, knows that harvesting grapes is a big deal in wine country. France has the perfect climate to grow top-rate grapes.

PARIS: A BIG-CITY SNAPSHOT

▲ **A STROLL IN PARIS**
It's hard to stroll down this Parisian street without taking you eyes off the Eiffel Tower. This world-famous monument offers a must-see view of the city. Race you to the top!

There is always something to do or to see in Paris, the City of Light. Paris is split in two by a river named the Seine. Many bridges cross the river, so it is easy to get around. Paris is the capital of France.

The Right Bank

Begin your sightseeing at the Arc de Triomphe. It is a huge arch that sits in the middle of a busy intersection. Napoleon started building the arch to celebrate his triumph in battle. Today, the Arc de Triomphe **commemorates** France's fallen soldiers.

Next, head to the Louvre. Once a king's palace, this is one of the biggest and most famous art museums in the world. The Louvre's most famous painting is the *Mona Lisa*, by Leonardo da Vinci. It is kept in a heavily protected display case. If you want to see this painting, be prepared for crowds. It is usually mobbed.

DOWNTOWN ▶
Paris is often called "the city of love."

Across the River

Each of Paris's many bridges across the Seine has its own charm. Each offers its own unique views. To start, head to the Left Bank across the Pont D'Arcole. It will take you to an island in the Seine called Ile de la Cité. This island is home to Paris's most famous church, Notre Dame Cathedral. Its construction began in 1163 and took 200 years to complete. Inside, you can see where Napoleon crowned himself emperor in 1804.

The Left Bank

Paris's Left Bank is home to the University of Paris and to the Panthéon, nearby. This huge, domed building is a monument to France's great thinkers. It is also where many of France's great thinkers are buried.

To the west you will find the Jardins du Luxembourg. Its gardens and perfect lawns are set in the shadow of the French Senate building. You might see some of France's leaders there. Luxembourg Gardens is filled with chairs and benches—a good place to enjoy a picnic.

From the Jardins du Luxembourg you can see the top of the Eiffel Tower. This landmark was constructed in 1889 to commemorate the Revolution and to show off French engineering skills. The tower shocked Parisians back then. They thought it was awful. Today, people love it. Make sure to go to the top. The view is unreal.

LOVING THE LOUVRE ▶
The Louvre is one of the most famous museums in the world. It is home to the lovely *Mona Lisa*.

PARIS'S TOP-10 CHECKLIST

If you are heading to Paris, here is a list of the top 10 things you have to do:

☐ Visit the Grave of the Unknown Soldier at the Arc de Triomphe.

☐ Walk down the Champs Elysées.

☐ Check out modern art at the Centre Pompidou.

☐ Go window-shopping at the fabulous Right Bank Shops.

☐ Wander around the Louvre looking at art. Try to answer the age-old question: Why is the Mona Lisa smiling?

☐ Cross the famous bridges over the Seine River.

☐ Take a tour of Notre Dame Cathedral.

☐ Take a boat ride on the Seine. Wave to the tourists.

☐ Enjoy a picnic at the Jardins du Luxembourg.

☐ Ride the elevator to the top of the Eiffel Tower. Snap some photos.

4 TOP SIGHTS

Mont Saint Michel

Mont Saint Michel is a tiny coastal city built on an island with one tall, lonely hill. Actually, it is only an island for part of the day—when the tide is high. When the tide is low, it is a little town sitting above miles of wet sand.

This town's most impressive building is the abbey. An abbey is a place where Christian **monks** live and worship. The one at Mont Saint Michel is huge and sits at the top of the hill. Construction on Mont Saint Michel started in A.D. 708. The really impressive parts were built in the 11th and 12th centuries, when the Abbey Church was begun.

Below the abbey, where monks still live today, is the main street of Mont Saint Michel. In fact, it is the island's only street, called the Grand Rue. It is filled with shops, restaurants, and even hotels.

If you can, stay the night so you can continue your exploring and watch the tides do their magic, turning a tiny town into an enchanted island.

▲ SAND CASTLE
Above, what looks like a fairy-tale castle is really an abbey—a place where Christian monks lived. Parts of this fortress were built in 1137.

Versailles

In 1789, revolution broke out in France. The lower and middle classes grew tired of rich people taking their money and wasting it on **luxury**. If you are curious to see such luxury, head to Versailles (say vair-SIGH).

King Louis XIV built the royal palace of Versailles in 1678. Inside you will find fabulous (and sometimes tacky) **décor**. Check out the Hall of Mirrors with its huge **chandeliers**. Or stop by Louis XIV's private chapel. Then step outside to see the gardens. Versailles is famous for its perfect lawns, huge fountains, and rare flowers.

▲ HALL OF MIRRORS
This room seems to go on forever and ever. With an endless line of huge mirrors and chandeliers, the Hall of Mirrors is quite a sight.

▲ THE ROYAL PALACE
This national treasure was once home to the kings of France. Louis XIV converted it from a hunting lodge to a full spread with gardens and all. Versailles is now a national museum.

Cannes

Do you prefer the beach to museums and ancient castles? Then head to Cannes, on the Mediterranean Sea.

Start your tour by walking down the Boulevard de la Croisette. This is the best place to people-watch. Check out the shops and watch the yachts come in and out. Dream about owning one. Maybe one day you will!

Next, head to the beaches. Maybe you will spot one of the movie stars that hang out in Cannes. Don't be surprised if you place your towel next to Jennifer Lopez.

If you happen to be in Cannes in May, you're in luck! This is when the famous Cannes Film Festival takes place. Some say that an award from the Cannes Film Festival is better than an Oscar.

▲ EVENING IN CANNES
When you're done rubbing shoulders with the rich and famous, you might want to go for a stroll. There is a lot to see in Cannes.

▼ FILM FESTIVAL

Winning an award at the Cannes Film Festival is a huge honor. Actors and directors from around the world flock to Cannes each May for the festival.

Du 10 au 21 mai

CANNES2000

53ème Festival International du Film

Chamonix and Mont Blanc

Chamonix and Mont Blanc are located in the Alps near Switzerland. People in this part of the world love to eat cheese fondue. That is where you dip pieces of bread in a pot of melted cheese. It is a great snack after a long day of hiking around the foothills of Mont Blanc. So what will you see while you are building up your appetite? Well, to begin with, the town of Chamonix is like a little Paris-in-the-mountains. The towns look different, but they are both exciting.

Try to make it to Chamonix in the winter. You can spend the day on some of the best ski slopes in the world. If you go in the summer, you can explore the many trails that line the surrounding mountains. The easiest way to get to some of these trails is by cable car. Cable cars will take you high into the mountains for a fantastic view of Mont Blanc, the highest peak in France. If you want to climb Mont Blanc, you'd better start training now. Only the world's best mountain climbers can make it to the top of this mountain.

CHAIRLIFT AT MONT BLANC ▶
You can take a chairlift up Mont
Blanc. This is the highest peak
in the European Alps.

▼ RIVER ARVE IN CHAMONIX
Surrounded by small shops
and restaurants, you can get
your fill of French life from the
riverbank.

GOING TO SCHOOL IN FRANCE

France has one of the best educational systems in the world. French kids start at age 5 and can leave at 16. Most continue to age 18. When students turn 15, they make a decision about what they want to do with their lives. Some choose vocational school, where they learn trades such as auto repair or plumbing. Other students work to pass an exam called the Baccalauréat. You must pass your "bac" if you want to go to college.

Around 15% of students in France attend private schools. These schools are often religious.

▲ A FRENCH CLASSROOM
These French students learn many of the same subjects as you —math, science, social studies. Classes are taught in French.

FRENCH SPORTS

France's number-one sport is definitely soccer. Go to any small town in France and you are sure to find a local team's soccer stadium. The French have a great national soccer team—they won the World Cup in 2000, a feat most countries only dream about.

Bicycling is another popular French sport. Each year France holds the Tour de France. It is a bike race through the towns and countryside that lasts for three weeks. In the biking world, this is the most important event of the year.

The French also love tennis. Every summer they host a tennis competition called the French Open. It is one of the most important tennis tournaments in the world.

▲ BICYCLE RACING
The Tour de France is the most famous bike race in the world! Cyclists from all over the world come to France to compete in it.

FROM FARMING TO FACTORIES

France has one of the strongest economies on the planet. The French produce cars, medicines, wine, and electronics. These industries employ millions of workers, and their products are sold all over the world.

Food production is a very important industry. Farmers grow crops and raise animals. Small factories are also involved in the food business. These factories make everything from wine to cheese to cookies. French wine is world-famous, and people will pay many francs for a good bottle. The French franc is the type of money used in France.

France's **natural resources** include oil, wood, and metals. Workers help to find these resources and prepare them for **export**.

Many French people work in the tourist industry. They run the hotels and restaurants that take care of tourists when they come to visit. That means when you order dinner in France, you are helping the French economy. So eat as much as you can. It's all for a good cause!

FRENCH CHEESES ▶
Wine and cheese is a perfect combination. In France, making cheese is an art form. Did you know that cheese is a common breakfast item in France?

▲ HARVESTING GRAPES
Handy wicker baskets make grape collecting easier. These grape pickers work through the day. They harvest the best in the bunch.

THE FRENCH GOVERNMENT

France is a democracy. That means that the people vote to elect their leaders.

France has a president, who is elected directly by the voters. The president's term lasts for seven years. The president works closely with the Assemblée Nationale, which makes the laws in France. There are 577 members of the Assemblée Nationale elected by the members' home provinces. This term lasts for five years.

France also has a senate, which has 321 members. The people do not elect these senators. Regional governments choose them. The senate does not have much power. It serves mostly to advise the national government.

France is also divided into 101 departments, which are like small states. Each department has its own local government. Local governments work closely with France's national government.

FRANCE'S NATIONAL FLAG

The flag has three panels—red, white, and blue. The red and blue are traditional colors of Paris. The red may represent Saint Denis, the patron saint of Paris, and the blue, Saint Martin, who wore a blue coat that he gave to a beggar (a symbol of charity). The white represents the purity of the Virgin Mary and Joan of Arc, and is the color of royalty in France.

Between 75% and 80% of French people are Roman Catholic. Catholics are Christians. They follow the teachings of Jesus found in the New Testament of the Bible. Catholics are different from other Christians because they also follow the teachings of the Pope, a religious leader who lives near Rome, Italy. About 2% of French people are Protestants. Protestants are also Christians, but they do not follow the Pope's teachings.

Muslims make up about 3% of the French population. Muslims follow the teachings of Mohammed that are found in their holy book, called the Koran. Many French Muslims are from African countries like Algeria and Tunisia, where France once had colonies.

In addition, Jews make up about 1% of the French population. They follow the teachings of the Torah found in the Old Testament of the Bible.

◄ GOTHIC CHURCH
Gothic design is an old way of making buildings. The Chartres Cathedral follows this traditional style. There are many beautiful cathedrals all over France.

FRENCH FOOD

French food is some of the best in the world. It has influenced cooking all over the globe. You can probably just look around your house to find French food, such as French fries (pommes frites—say PUM FREET) and French toast (pain d'or—say PAN DOR).

What do people like to eat in France? Well, cheese is probably at the top of the list. The French make hundreds of different kinds of cheeses. Brie and camembert are among the most popular.

French people often eat cheese at the end of dinner. What do they eat before that? They might start with soup. One popular soup is consommé, a kind of meat broth. Another is vichyssoise, which is cold potato and leek soup. The main course often includes meat in a **gourmet** sauce, a vegetable, and a starchy food, such as potato. The French will also definitely have their wonderful bread, and they enjoy their green salads after the main course.

French desserts include ice cream or various mouth-watering cakes and pies. Mousse is a well-known French dessert. It is like a creamy pudding.

◀ FROG'S LEGS
All cooked up, you may not be able to tell these are frog's legs. This tasty dish is a French specialty. Some say they taste just like chicken!

DOUBLE-THICK CHOCOLATE MOUSSE

Ingredients:

2 cups chocolate chips

2 large eggs

2 tsp vanilla extract

2 cups heavy cream, heated

WARNING:
**Never cook or bake by yourself.
Always have an adult assist you
in the kitchen.**

Directions:

Put the cream in a saucepan and heat on low. Place the chocolate chips, the eggs, and the vanilla in a food processor. Mix for about half a minute.

When the cream is hot, slowly add it to the food processor while continuing to mix. Stop mixing when the chocolate mixture is smooth and the chocolate chips are perfectly blended. Next, pour the chocolate mixture into small bowls and refrigerate. The mousse is ready to serve as soon as it has become solid.

UP CLOSE: CORSICA

Corsica is the third-largest island in the Mediterranean Sea. Its area is about 3,350 square miles (8,680 sq km). It has nearly 625 miles (1,000 km) of beautiful, sunny coastline. The mountains in the center of the island have snow on them.

Corsica is close to Italy. Over the years, Italian kingdoms claimed the island as their own. In the year 1768, Corsica was sold to the French for 40 million francs. Of course, many Corsicans were not happy about being bought and sold. There are still some people in Corsica who want independence. Many Corsicans, however, are happy to be part of France.

Corsica's claim to fame is as the birthplace of Napoleon, who became emperor of France in 1804. At the height of his power, Napoleon controlled most of Western Europe.

Hiking, Swimming, and Exploring

Corsica has one of the largest national parks in Europe. It is called Parc Naturel Régional de Corse and it covers about half the island. The park stretches from the beaches inland to Corsica's highest peak, Monte Cinto. This peak reaches almost 9,000 feet (about 2,700 m). Frà Li Monti is the name of one of the most popular hiking trails through this park. It crosses several mountains and is about 100 miles (161 km) long!

▲ CASTLE IN THE SKY
Castles are no strange sight in Corsica. This castle in Corte makes for a great photo opportunity.

Corsica's Towns and Villages

Corsica is a great place to visit because parts of it have not changed for hundreds of years. Narrow, winding streets surround ancient churches in the villages. Fortresses loom high above every settlement.

Bastia is a booming **port** town in the north of Corsica. It was built under a 16th-century fortress. Be sure to check out the huge open-air market near the Hôtel de Ville (town hall). You can pick up goat cheese and olives for your hike up Monte Cinto.

Corte is a city is in the center of Corsica, high in Corsica's uplands. The University of Corsica is located in Corte, so the city remains at the center of Corsican culture. If you visit Corte, check out the 15th-century fortress built into the side of the cliffs. If you feel like shopping, head to the Cours Paoli. There are plenty of little stores to keep you entertained.

Ajaccio, in southern Corsica, may be the most famous city on the island. It is the birthplace of the most famous Corsican—Napoleon Bonaparte. One thing is for sure: if you visit Ajaccio, you will not forget he was born here! Streets, towers, **shrines**, everything seems to be named after Napoleon. Of course, that's one of the best reasons to visit Ajaccio. You can learn all about France's most famous dictator by visiting places like his childhood home and the Napoleon Museum. Then you can take a break to enjoy fabulous napoleons (pastries named after you-know-who) on one of Ajaccio's busiest streets— Cours Napoleon.

▼ NAPOLEON PASTRY
Corsica is the birthplace of France's greatest general, Napoleon Bonaparte. This pastry is called a napoleon.

FASCINATING FACT

Napoleon...great leader or great pastry? The answer is both. Why is there a pastry called a napoleon? Rumor has it that this puff pastry was created by a Danish royal pastry chef. He came up with it in the 1800s to honor the French leader Napoleon Bonaparte.

HOLIDAYS

The French people celebrate many national and religious holidays. Bastille Day, July 14, is the most significant national holiday. It celebrates the beginning of the French Revolution in 1789. Armistice Day, or Remembrance Day, is November 11. It honors French soldiers, especially those who fought in World Wars I and II. Also important is May Day on May 1. May Day honors French workers.

Many of the major holidays in France are Christian. The most important is Christmas (or Nöel in French). Nöel celebrates the birth of Jesus. Easter is another important religious holiday in France. It commemorates Jesus' death.

▲ BASTILLE DAY PARADE
This celebration is like an Independence Day parade. There are lots of music, patriotic uniforms, and French flags.

LEARNING THE LANGUAGE

English	French	How to say it
Hello	bonjour	bon-JHOOR
Good bye	Au revoir	OH rev-WAHR
How are you	Comment allez-vous?	ko-MOT AH-lay VOO
My name is	Je m'appelle	JHEH mah-PELL
Please	S'il vous plait	SEE VOO PLAY
Thank you	merci	MEHR-see
Excuse me	excusez-moi	ek-SKYOO-say MWAH

QUICK FACTS

FRANCE

Capital ▶
Paris

Borders
English Channel (N)
Belgium,
Luxembourg,
Germany,
Switzerland,
Italy (E)
Mediterranean Sea, Spain (S)
Atlantic Ocean (W)

Area
176,460 square miles
(547,030 sq km)

Population
59,329,691

Largest Cities
Paris (2,152,423 people)
Marseilles (800,000)
Lyons (415,487)
Toulouse (358,688)

▼ **Main Religious Groups**

Roman Catholic
80%

Other 14%

Muslim 3%

Protestant 2%

Jewish 1%

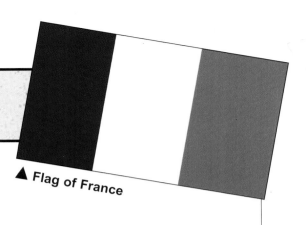

▲ Flag of France

Coastline ▶
2,130 miles (3,427 km)

Longest River
Loire
634 miles (1,020 km)

Literacy Rate
99% of all French
people can read

Major Industries
Steel, machinery, chemicals,
automobiles

Chief Crops
Cereals, sugarbeets,
potatoes, wine grapes,
beef, dairy products, fish

Natural Resources
Coal, iron, ore, bauxite,
fish, timber

◀ **Monetary Unit**
French franc and
Euro

PEOPLE TO KNOW

◀ Sophie Marceau

Sophie Marceau was born in Paris, France, in 1966. She started acting at the young age of 14 and became very popular with her first film. Born Sophie Maupu, she changed her name to Marceau just before the release of her first runaway French hit, *La Boum*. Sophie who has recently started on English language films, has worked with Mel Gibson, David Spade, and other famous Americans.

Jacques Cousteau ▶

Jacques Cousteau amazed the world with his underwater adventures. He brought the undersea world to television with specially built cameras and boats. He also invented the scuba tank, for breathing under water.

◀ Joan of Arc

One of France's most important people, Joan of Arc helped defend France from the invading English. The English eventually captured her and burned her at the stake, but not before she had saved France. She died in 1431, when she was only 19 years old.

MORE TO READ

Want to know more about France? Check out these books.

Dahl, Michael S. *Countries of the World: France*. Mankato, MN: Capstone Press, Inc.,1988.
Discover all that France has to offer through photos and facts.

Ganeri, Anita, Wright, Rachel, and Shackell, John. *Country Topics for Crafts Projects: France*. Danbury, CT: Franklin Watts, Inc., 1995.
Do fun arts and crafts projects that relate to France.

Green, Robert. *Vive La France: The French Resistance During WWII*. Danbury, CT: Franklin Watts, Inc., 1997.
Tells the story of the brave French people who stood up to the Nazis during World War II.

Hoban, Sarah and Moulder, Bob. *Daily Life in Ancient and Modern Paris*. Minneapolis, MN: The Lerner Publishing Group, 2000.
Take a look at what daily life was like throughout history in France.

Stein, Richard Conrad. *Cities of the World: Paris*. Danbury, CT: Children's Press, 1997.
Offers a more complete look at the great city of Paris.

Wright, Nicola and Wooley, Kim. *Getting to Know France and French*. Hauppauge, NY: Barron's Educational Series, Inc., 1993.
Learn about the land, people, and language in this colorful book.

GLOSSARY

Alliance (uh-LYE-unce)—an agreement made between countries to work together

Ancestors (AN-sess-turz)—a person's older relatives who are no longer living

Chandeliers (shan-duh-LEERZ)—large, fancy, hanging light fixtures

Commemorates (kuh-MEM-uh-rates)—does something special to honor someone or something

Décor (day-KOR)—the style used to decorate a room or space

Dynasties (DYE-nuh-steez)—rulers from the same family who are in power one after another

Economic depression (ee-kuh-NOM-ik di-PRESH-uhn)—a period of time when businesses do badly and people cannot make any money

Equator (i-KWAY-tur)—an imaginary line around the middle of Earth, halfway between the North and South poles

Export (EK-sport)—to send products to another country for trade or sale

Foreign (FOR-in)—from another country

Gourmet (goor-MAY)—especially delicious, carefully prepared

Guillotine (GHEE-uh-teen)—a machine used during the French Revolution to chop off a person's head

Impressionism (im-PRESH-uhn-izm)—a style of painting in which the artist shows how the subject looks at a certain moment

Luxury (LUHK-shuh-ree)—something purchased for pleasure and not out of need

Monks (MUHNGKS)—men who live away from society and devote their lives to their religion

Natural resources (NATCH-er-uhl REE-zor-sez)— materials such as trees, metals, and wildlife that a country uses to make what its people need

Port (PORT)—a city where ships can safely dock to load and unload cargo

Revolution (RE-ah-LOO-shun)—a movement to overthrow the government that can be violent

Shrines (SHRINEZ)—buildings or monuments that are considered sacred or holy

Stable (STAY-buhl)—unchanging

Vegetation (vej-uh-TAY-shuhn)—plant life

INDEX